THE
MAKING
of
ST. JEROME

THE
MAKING
of
ST. JEROME

MARIE BEATH BADIAN

PLAYWRIGHTS CANADA PRESS

TORONTO

The Making Of St. Jerome © 2017 by Marie Beath Badian

LIBRARY AND ARCHIVES CANADA CATALOGUING IN PUBLICATION
Badian, Marie Beath, author
   The making of St. Jerome / Marie Beath Badian.

A play.
Issued in print and electronic formats.
ISBN 978-1-77091-738-5 (softcover).--ISBN 978-1-77091-739-2 (PDF).
--ISBN 978-1-77091-740-8 (HTML).--ISBN 978-1-77091-741-5 (Kindle)

   I. Title.

PS8603.A33442M34 2017   C812'.6   C2016-907654-7
                                      C2016-907655-5

We acknowledge the financial support of the Canada Council for the Arts, the Ontario Arts Council (OAC), the Ontario Media Development Corporation, and the Government of Canada through the Canada Book Fund for our publishing activities.

 Canada Council for the Arts   Conseil des arts du Canada

ONTARIO ARTS COUNCIL
CONSEIL DES ARTS DE L'ONTARIO
an Ontario government agency
un organisme du gouvernement de l'Ontario

Ontario Media Development Corporation

This play is dedicated to Manoy.

PLAYWRIGHT'S NOTES

This is a fictionalized play inspired by real-life events.

On May 21, 2004,
Seventeen-year-old Jeffrey Reodica
Was shot by a plainclothes police officer.
This event is the inspiration and catalyst of this play.

This is not a linear play.
It is both present and past.
Time moves on and time stands still.
These changes in time are indicated by
Shift or *Rewind.*

Action described is intended to by physicalized.
Use of projection would be ideal but not necessary.
Words in Tagalog are peppered throughout.

A forward slash (/) = the line is overlapped or cut off by the following line.
Italics are used to highlight Tagalog.

Scene titles may be used as text, with subtlety, at the discretion of the director.

GLOSSARY OF TERMS

Adobo: A Filipino dish of chicken or pork stewed in vinegar, garlic, soy sauce, bay leaves, and peppercorns.

Anak: Child.

Ate: A Tagalog term of respect for an older female sibling.

Debut: A debutante ball, celebrated by some Filipino families on the occasion of a daughter's eighteenth birthday. The "t" is silent.

Kuya: A Tagalog term of respect for an older male sibling.

Lumpia: Filipino-style egg rolls.

Sabaw: Soup.

Sinigang: Filipino sour soup.

SIU: Special Investigations Unit. The SIU is a civilian law enforcement agency. Independent of the police, the SIU investigates circumstances involving police and civilians that have resulted in serious injury or death.

Tito: Uncle.

The Making of St. Jerome premiered as part of the Next Stage Theatre Festival at Factory Studio Theatre, Toronto, from January 6 to January 17, 2010, with the following cast and creative team:

Jason De Jesus: Byron Abalos
Jerome De Jesus / Chorus 4: Christian Feliciano
Chorus 1: Keith Barker
Chorus 2: Aura Carcueva
Chorus 3: Audrey Dwyer

Director: Nina Lee Aquino
Stage Manager: Kat Chin
Set and Costume Design: Jackie Chau
Sound Design: Romeo Candido
Assistant Sound Designer: Kevin Centeno
Choreography: Clare Preuss
Lighting Design: Aaron Kelly
Co-Producers: Renna Reddie and Colin Doyle

CHARACTERS

Jason De Jesus: twenty-two years old, *Kuya*

Jerome De Jesus: seventeen years old, little brother

Chorus [two men, two women]: ever-present and relentless

As a group they are:

Family, Medical Staff, the News

Individually they are:

Chorus 1 [man]: Father, Officer X, Father Williamson, Dean, Paul, Police Chief

Chorus 2 [woman]: Mother, Irene, Girl, Anchor

Chorus 3 [woman]: Julie, Tess, Reporter

Chorus 4 [man—same actor who plays Jerome]: Lawyer, Vince

SETTING

Jason's bedroom—4 a.m., June 2006.

The eve of the final day of the coroner's inquest into Jerome's death.

PROLOGUE: IN SLEEP WE DREAM OF BETTER TIMES

JASON is dreaming. JEROME, age nine, appears, reading out loud his grade four assignment on heroes.

JEROME   What is a hero?
Does he save the day?
Does he leap tall buildings in a single bound?
Does he always get the bad guy?
Sometimes,
But not always.
I have a hero.
And he is my brother, Jason.
He taught me that even though
I'm small,
I can walk tall,
I can shoot ball
Better than those other kids.
We play video games,
We wrestle,
We laugh.
He told me,
Dream big
And if I work hard
I can be anything I want to be.
Anything.

SCENE 1: INSOMNIA

JASON's room. A basement bedroom. He jolts up from sleep. He is at a desk in front of a computer. The number twenty-seven is projected.

JASON   I can't sleep.
I haven't.
I don't know how long it's been.

Well, that's a lie.
I slip into sleep.
Sometimes . . .
For ten minutes or whatever.

In a few hours, the coroner's inquest will reconvene.
And a panel of strangers will make a recommendation.

So, I don't have time for real sleep.
The letters, the emails, the phone calls keep pouring in.
Gotta read them. Gotta respond.

CHORUS 1   This is *The Star*.

CHORUS 2   *The Sun.*

CHORUS 3   *The Globe.*

JASON   Two years after the fact,
On the eve of what will finally be the truth,
The whole fucking universe wants to know the same
thing—

CHORUS   Tell us about your brother.

       JASON sighs.

JASON   He played the sax,
Worked at Tim Hortons.
He was a joker,
A pretty good ball player,
For 5'4",
An altar boy,
Mom's pride and joy /

CHORUS   Tell us the truth.

JASON   As if they really care.
They don't give two shits about a real story.
All they want is a sound bite to butcher into a juicy
headline—

CHORUS 1   DEATH OF A SCHOOLBOY.

CHORUS 2   FAMILY CRIES FOUL.

CHORUS 3   CONFLICT CLOUDS THE TRUTH.

JASON   But *you* care, right? That's why you log in every day.
          Sometimes twice a day, right?
          Sixty thousand hits and counting.

          The projected twenty-seven seconds begins to count-down. It is never actually twenty-seven seconds. It is much slower. JEROME *appears;* JASON *does not notice him.*

          Because of your captive and unfaltering dedication, I'm going to tell you a story. The true story about two brothers. Don't worry. I'm not going to get Biblical on you.

CHORUS   Tell us the truth.

JASON   Teenagers. Jason and Jerome. Three years apart. First came me and then came Jerome. You probably heard it all before. Grew up as friends. Best friends. Up until grade four at least. In grade four, Jerome had to do a project on heroes and he wrote about me.

JEROME   What is a hero?

JASON   But then we hit high school and boom, we hate each other's guts. It happens.

JEROME   I have a hero—

JASON   I mean, for real, what freak asshole brothers wouldn't hate each other's guts?

JEROME   My brother Jason.

JASON   Separate ways. Separate interests. I think Jerome chose band cuz I was already playing ball. We never talked about it, it just worked out. Who wants their punk-ass little brother on their team? C'mon.

Don't judge me.

A phone rings. At first faint but grows louder.

You know the story. It's you. Don't tell me you say—

**JASON /
JEROME**   Hey, *Kuya*!

JASON   —in the halls. You ignore each other. Like the plague. Admit it. But, you grow out of it. Everybody does.

JEROME   Hey, *Kuya*!

JASON   You go to university. You choose Western—because it's away from home but close enough to visit. The first few weeks are awesome, but slowly you start to miss home. At first, you miss the washing machine. Next, you long for the privacy of your room in the basement. Then, you crave Mom's chicken *adobo* with *sabaw* on the rice. You start to miss your big sister, then maybe your nephew. And then you get so restless—

Shift. JASON *is on the phone with* JEROME.

Hey, Jer, wanna come up for a visit this weekend? I know this pub off campus that doesn't card.

JEROME   Sweet, *Kuya*! I'll show all those Western honeys where it's at! Scarborough Reprezent!

JASON   And you spring for his bus ticket, because you get a student discount. You bring him to Ye Olde Boot, because it sounds worldly. You are the only two brown people in the place.

JASON /
JEROME   What the fuck is this music?

JASON   And you bond, man. Brotherly bond.

JEROME   Thanks for the weekend, *Kuya*. It was cool.

JASON   A month later, you go home for Christmas and he says—

JASON /
JEROME   Hey, *Kuya*, Merry Christmas.

JASON   And he gives you a present: a mint-condition, first pressing of Public Enemy's *Fight the Power*—just like the one he scratched two years ago.

JEROME   Do you like it? It was so hard to find. I checked on eBay but people wanted so much for it. Finally I bought it off Dean. I didn't ask him where he got it. It's probably hot. But, anyway.

JASON   Wow, Jer . . .

JEROME   I'm really sorry I scratched it. I . . . just wanted to try out your gear. That's all. I didn't want to wreck it or anything. You just got so mad that I scratched it. You totally lost your shit. Like as if I meant to do it.

JASON   I know you didn't mean /

JEROME	I didn't mean to do it. Only a dick would mean to do it. I know you think I'm a dick most of the time. But serious, *Kuya*—
JASON	Thanks, dick.

JASON and JEROME hug.

It's your story, isn't it?
Well, fuck you.
Cuz it's not mine.
It's fiction—
A fairy tale,
A dream.
No Western,
No pub,
No Merry Christmas,
None of it happens.

CHORUS	TELL US THE TRUTH!

JASON answers the phone. Transition. It is the past.

JASON	Hello?
TESS	Jay, where the hell are you?
JASON	I'm stuck in traffic.
TESS	What? What time did you leave?
JASON	Late. I got into a fight with Jer.
TESS	Again?

JASON   Call the club and tell them that we're just outside looking for parking.

TESS   Jay, don't make me lie to them. It's bad business. It took me forever to book you this gig.

JASON   Jesus, Tess, it's not lying, it's buying time. Later.

TESS   But, Jay /

JASON   Later.

JASON grabs a box of records and a turntable case, about to leave. The phone rings again.

Jesus, Tess, what?
Uh, sorry, yes, this is Jason De Jesus.
Yeah, I'm his brother. Why? What did he do now?

Oh God.

The timer reaches zero.

Pop. Pop. Pop.

SCENE 2: HAPPY BIRTHDAY

The past. A restaurant.

FAMILY   *[singing]* . . . Happy Birthday, dear Jerome—

JASON   Two weeks before the altercation—

FAMILY	Happy Birthday to you!
JASON	—my brother turned seventeen.

The family applauds as JEROME *blows out his candles.*

FATHER	I would like to make a toast!

The rest of the family groans.

Jerome, son, your mom and I are proud of you. You work hard and hard work pays off.

JASON	Translation—your brother Jason is lazy.
FATHER	You will be the first one in this family to go to university.
JASON	Translation—I still can't get over that your big sister got knocked up when she turned nineteen and that your big brother thinks that playing records is a career.
JEROME	I haven't gotten any acceptance letters yet, Pa.
MOTHER	You will, *Anak.*
FATHER	And because of your hard work, your mom and I want to give you this.

He hands JEROME *an envelope.*

JEROME	*[opening envelope]* Holy shit.
MOTHER	*Ssut.* Watch your language!

JASON /
JULIE   What is it?

JEROME   A seven day Contiki tour of Europe!

JASON /
JULIE   Holy shit.

MOTHER   *Sssut!*

JASON   Classic. I'm not bitter; I'm just saying. When Julie turned eighteen she got a huge *debut* at the Embassy Suites in Markham with a cotillion, eighteen roses, and everything. Even an ice sculpture.

JEROME   Sweeeeeeeet!

JASON   When I turned eighteen, I got a cheque for a thousand bucks. I think Ma and Pa wanted me to use it for tuition or something, even though I didn't apply to any colleges.

FATHER   You deserve it, Son.

JASON   I used it to buy my decks and a shopping spree for vinyls with my best friend Paul. I scored *Fight the Power* with that cash.

JEROME   Thanks, Pa.

JASON   I guess in giving him such an extravagant present for his seventeenth birthday they were hoping to positively reinforce Jer's path to university.

FATHER   Thank your mother.

JEROME   Thanks, Ma.

JASON   I gotta go.

FATHER   Where are you going?

JASON   I'm DJing at a *debut* in Pickering.

JEROME   Sweet, *Kuya*. Can I crash?

JASON   No.

MOTHER   Jason. Let him come. He can practise driving on the way
              there.

JEROME   Yeah, *Kuya*, then you can drink!

JASON   It's not a party, Ma. It's work.

FATHER   *[scoffing]* Work.

JEROME   S'okay, *Kuya*. It's cool.

JASON   Or at least that's what I think he said. I was in such a rush
              to get out of there.

JEROME   S'okay, *Kuya*. Fuck you.

JASON   Memory is such a fucked-up thing. Some things you try
              really hard to remember. Some things you never ever
              forget. Ever.

SCENE 3: IT'S NOT WHAT YOU THINK

The sound of an ambulance. The past.

JASON   I'm Jason De Jesus. I'm looking for my brother. They said he was here . . .

MEDICAL
STAFF   Jerome De Jesus?
           Your brother?

JASON   Yeah. I mean. Yes. Where is he? What happened? I want to see him.

MEDICAL
STAFF   I'm sorry.
           You can't see him just yet.

JASON   Why? What's going on?

MEDICAL
STAFF   Your brother was involved in an altercation.

JASON   What do you mean, altercation?

MEDICAL
STAFF   Your brother has been shot.

JASON   Full stop here. Just in case you don't know. Like, there's a possibility you're new to this website and you don't happen to read newspapers or watch the news or care about the world or whatever.

ANCHOR   Shots fired in an east end neighbourhood.
One youth rushed to hospital.

JASON   Kids get shot all the time, right? Like it's practically not
even the lead item on the news anymore, especially if the
kid had the misfortune of living at Neilson and McLevin
or Jane and Finch or something.

ANCHOR   And now the weather—

CHORUS 4   Sports—

CHORUS 3   Entertainment—

CHORUS 1   Business—

JASON   Front page. That's reserved for pure innocence, man.
Like twelve-year-old kid shot in his own school or blonde
girl on Boxing Day.

Don't judge me. It's the truth.

**MEDICAL
STAFF**   Your brother has been shot.

JASON   I know what you're thinking—

CHORUS 3   Was he known to police?

CHORUS 2   What gang did he belong to?

CHORUS 4   What trouble was he in?

JASON   Don't deny it. It's conditioning, man. Truth? I thought
it too.

Shift.

I want to see him. NOW.

**MEDICAL
STAFF**   The SIU are investigating the altercation.

JASON   Hell ya, you heard right. The SIU.
Special Investigations Unit.
The cops who investigate cops.
That's right, a cop shot my brother.
And before you start jumping to conclusions, let me spare
you the effort.
That year:

THE NEWS   The police shot eight people.
De Jesus was the youngest.
The only one with no criminal record.
The only one who wasn't a drug dealer.
The only one who wasn't crazy.

JASON   Holy fuck. What happened?

DEAN   Jason?

JASON   Dean, what are you doing here?

DEAN   Jay, man, shit. I am so sorry. I was there. I mean, I was
right there.
Oh shit. I'm so sorry.

JASON   Jesus Christ, Dean! Tell me what happened!

DEAN   You don't know?

JASON	Fuck, Dean, tell me!
DEAN	Yesterday Vince got his teeth knocked out by a bunch of white guys on the ball court at Our Lady of Peace. They roughed him up and said, *Go back where you came from and eat your rice!* So a bunch of us went back there today after school to fight back. It was just supposed to be a fight, Jay. Just a fight.

SCENE 4: TO SERVE AND PROTECT

Twenty-seven seconds on the clock. It counts down slowly, not in real time.

CHORUS	VERSION ONE.
	The buzz went around school.
	The plan was to meet at the ball court behind
	Our Lady of Peace.
	There were only
	Two
	Four
	Six
	Eight
	Ten of us.
	Including Jer.
	Jer was only there to see the fights.
	We chased the guy who knocked Vince's teeth out,
	Cornered him,
	Then a car pulled up.
	Two huge white guys.
	We didn't know who they were.

No badge. No nothing.
One guy went up to Jer.
We thought he was the uncle of one of the white kids.

JEROME   Who are you?

OFFICER X   Drop the rock!

> *JEROME drops the rock.*

You think you're so tough, motherfucker?

> *OFFICER X slaps JEROME on the head.*

CHORUS
2 / 3   He was trying to get Jer onto his stomach.
And then I saw the handcuffs—
But I still didn't know it was the police.

JEROME   Get away from me!

> *JEROME swings out.*

CHORUS
2 / 3   It looked like he was trying to punch him.
And then—
It sounded like a cap gun.
POP! POP! POP!

SCENE 5: FUNERAL

The past. A church.

The MOURNERS sing.

MOURNERS   . . . Lamb of God, who takes away the sins of the world—

JASON   Two weeks after his seventeenth birthday—

MOURNERS   —grant us peace.

JASON   —I buried my brother.

FATHER
WILLIAM   Please be seated.

JASON   The funeral was at Our Lady of Peace—
The church next to the school,
Next to the basketball court
Where Jer was shot.

FATHER
WILLIAM   It is difficult to say goodbye. I baptized Jerome. Celebrated
his first Communion and confirmation. My heart mourns
with all of you. Brothers and sisters, it is in times like these
when our faith in God is truly tested. We think, "How can
an all-loving and forgiving God take away someone so
young, so promising; such a loyal and obedient servant?"
Friends, as senseless as Jerome's death is, as we struggle to
understand God's purpose in this tragedy, rejoice in the

knowledge that Jerome is surely in the comfort and love of Jesus Christ.

And one day we will see him again.

MOURNERS /
JASON   Amen.

FATHER
WILLIAM   Jerome's friends would like to share some thoughts with you.

VINCE   He was a real good guy. A real good guy. He didn't start with anyone, y'know? He was just one of those real good guys. A guy you could just pick up the phone and call, y'know? He was always joking around, yo. Funny. Never stopped joking. Talented.

IRENE   The amazing thing about Jer was that he could sense when any of us were angry. He knew how to pacify us with his tender words.

JASON   Oh, come on.

IRENE   Jer was deeply spiritual. He was an active member of Youth for Christ—

JASON   He quit that two years ago.

IRENE   —and when things were really bad for me last year and I called Jer up and told him that I wanted to kill myself: he talked me out of it. Jer was my light and saviour during my darkest hour. Jer died because he cares—cared—for us so much. Every night before I go to bed, I pray to Jer to continue to look out for me. He is my guardian angel.

JASON   *[laughing]* Oh God.

FATHER
WILLIAM   And now some reflections from Jerome's brother, Jason.

JULIE   Jason, go. They're waiting.

JASON   *Ate*, I can't.

JULIE   Are you . . . laughing?

JASON   No.

JULIE   I can't believe you. Go. Everyone is staring.

JASON   I know. It's hilarious.

JULIE   Jason!

JASON   Can you go instead? Please, *Ate*. Tell them . . . um . . . just say—

JULIE   I can talk for myself, Jason. Pull yourself together.

JULIE stands and speaks to the congregation.

Umm. Hi. I'm Jer's sister, Julie. Umm . . . Well, as most of you probably know, Jer loved video games. Loved them. Like he was permanently attached to that Xbox, right? My son Ryan loved playing on that Xbox with his *Tito* Jer. He loved doing everything with his *Tito* Jer. Jer was really the only father Ryan knew.

A few weeks before Jer . . . passed, he really got into some new game. I dunno what it was called. *Grand . . . Theft . . . Halo*? He was on that thing as soon as he rolled out of bed and as soon as he got home from school. I had to yell at him to help me out, to get Ryan dressed, you know, *Tito* Jer stuff. He totally gave me attitude, even said, "*Ate* do it yourself." It was so unlike him. So distant. But he eventually turned the game off.

That game looked like such a stupid waste of time. But I know, now, that the real message, the reason he was pulling away from us, acting all distant and stuff, was that Ryan and I would need to get used to being on our own. You were the best, Jer. No one can ever replace you.

JASON   And there you have it, ladies and gentleman.
                  I'm not only a shit brother, I'm a shit uncle too.

SCENE 6: THE LIST

The present. JASON's *room.*

CHORUS   The truth,
                The truth,
                Tell us the truth.

JASON   This inquest is fucking me up. I try to sleep. I really try. I started trying to count down from a hundred. But by the time I reached twenty-seven I was so fucken depressed that I kept upping the countdown. I stopped counting backwards when I upped the ante to something like two thousand. I kept getting distracted. I'd get to, I don't know,

101 and start thinking about those crazy lists like *101 Uses for a Dead Cat* or *101 Places to Visit Before You Die*. And then I get to thinking of like *101 Reasons How Jer Could Still Be Alive . . .* like . . .

CHORUS ONE

JEROME What if—

JASON The white kids didn't pick a fight with the Filipino kids on the ball court.

CHORUS TWO

JEROME What if—

JASON The Flips didn't retaliate.

CHORUS THREE

JEROME What if—

JASON The cops never showed up.

CHORUS FOUR

JEROME What if—

JASON Jer stayed home.

CHORUS FIVE

JEROME What if—

JASON The cop identified himself.

CHORUS   SIX

JEROME   What if—

JASON   He hated basketball.

CHORUS   SEVEN

JEROME   What if—

JASON   There was no knife.

CHORUS   EIGHT

JEROME   What if—

JASON   Jer didn't try to run away.

CHORUS   NINE

JEROME   What if—

JASON   His school didn't close the music program.

CHORUS   TEN

JEROME   What if—

JASON   He didn't struggle.

CHORUS   ELEVEN

JEROME   What if—

JASON   The cops used pepper spray.

CHORUS   TWELVE

JEROME   What if—

JASON   The cop aimed at Jer's foot.

CHORUS   THIRTEEN

JEROME   What if—

JASON   I never found the record.

> As JEROME speaks, JASON starts counting to block out the memory.

JEROME   Shit.

JASON   FOURTEEN

JEROME   I didn't touch it.

JASON   FIFTEEN

JEROME   Who's lying?

JASON   SIXTEEN

JEROME   I don't know what you're talking about.

JASON   SEVENTEEN

JEROME   Maybe you left it there last night.

JASON   EIGHTEEN

JEROME	Okay.
JASON	NINETEEN
JEROME	It was me.
JASON	TWENTY
JEROME	I was just messing.
JASON	TWENTY-ONE
JEROME	Sorry, I gotta go.
JASON	TWENTY-TWO
JEROME	Hey, *Kuya*!
JASON	TWENTY-THREE
JEROME	Hey, *Kuya*!
JASON	TWENTY-FOUR
JEROME	Hey, *Kuya*!
JASON	TWENTY-FIVE
JEROME	Hey, *Kuya*!
JASON	TWENTY-SIX
JEROME	Hey, *Kuya*!

| JASON | TWENTY-SEVEN . . . twenty-seven . . . twenty-seven . . . I mean, the list could go on and on. There are a million and one "what ifs" . . . if you really think about it. |

SCENE 7: DUTY CALLS

The past. In the living room of the De Jesus home.

FATHER Murderers! Cold-blooded murderers! Liars!

JASON Two weeks after the shooting—

MOTHER They left my son bleeding on the street!

JASON —the Special Investigations Unit concluded that the cop was justified in shooting Jerome.

JULIE Ma, Pa, calm down, please. The newspapers are here. They want a statement.

JASON They said the entire altercation took twenty-seven seconds. It took twenty-seven seconds to engage Jerome and shoot him in the back three times.

FATHER You tell them that fat pig police officer murdered my Jerome. He will be punished!

MOTHER Why? Why are they here again? What more do they want? They are saying that Jerome was a gangster. A punk.

LAWYER You have to do it, Jason.

JASON	Do what?
LAWYER	Make a statement.
JASON	You're the lawyer.
LAWYER	Make a statement for your family.
JASON	No. Dad will. He just needs a minute.
LAWYER	He's too emotional. The papers will misrepresent your family. They'll make your father sound vindictive, irrational. You have to do it.
JASON	I can't. Ask Julie.
JULIE	I'll do it.
LAWYER	No. It can't be you.
JULIE	Why not?
LAWYER	I don't want to sound crass. But you're a very young woman and a single mother living with your parents in Scarborough. The media has enough fuel to perpetuate the stereotypes surrounding Jerome. And you don't want to drag your four-year-old son though this circus. It's enough that he has lost his uncle.
JULIE	Are you kidding me?
MOTHER	Jason, do this. Tell them. Tell them that your brother was a good boy. A good son. A good brother. Tell them. Please. Do it for Jer.

JASON   So I did it. For Jer.

         Transition. JASON *faces the media for the first time.*
         Focus is split between JASON *and his* FATHER *as he*
         instructs him.

FATHER   Tell them the truth.

JASON   I want to set the record straight about my brother, Jerome
         De Jesus.

FATHER   Tell them those pigs are liars.

JASON   My family is devastated by the findings of the SIU
         investigation.

FATHER   Tell them the SIU is just defending their friends.

JASON   We believe it is seriously flawed and—

FATHER   Tell them they are racists in uniforms.

JASON   . . . it has been positioned to protect the officers rather
         than the public.

FATHER   Tell them what goes around comes around.

JASON   We pledge that we will find out the truth of what happened
         that day.

MEDIA   *[simultaneously]* Tell us about your brother.

FATHER   *[simultaneously]* Tell them about your brother.

         This is the first time JASON *says this.*

JASON   Uh . . . He played the sax,
Worked at Tim Hortons.
He was a joker,
A pretty good ball player
for 5'4",
An altar boy,
Mom's pride and joy.
He had dreams of Europe,
Or the RCMP,
Or a personality on TV.

JEROME   What is a hero?

JASON   He loved video games.
He loved music and records,
And his family.

JEROME   I have a hero.

CHORUS   The truth.

JEROME   My brother, Jason.

JASON   He was my best friend.

SCENE 8: KUYA AT THE BUS STOP

The past. JASON and JEROME wait for the Lawrence East bus. JEROME goofs off and does his trademark "nose picking" to shock drivers while they pass. JASON, headphones on, ignores JEROME.

JEROME   Hey, *Kuya!*

JASON   Two days after his birthday—

JEROME   Yo, *Kuya!*

JASON   Don't talk to me.

JEROME   You're still pissed?

JASON ignores him.

I said I was sorry.

JASON   No, you didn't.

JEROME   Whatever.

JEROME spots a pimped-up car stopped at the lights.

Yo, guido, nice! Does your mom know that you did that to her car?

JASON   Shit. Jer. Stand at the corner and shut up. For once.

JEROME   I can't believe you're still pissed.

JASON   Oh you're right, Jer. Why should I still be pissed? Just because you happen to steal the car /

JEROME   I didn't steal it—

JASON   —and because I happened to be home, didn't know you took it /

JEROME   I told you—

JASON   —but still, I happened to be home, so I'M being punished because I didn't stop you.

JEROME   I asked you, *Kuya.*

JASON   No. You didn't.

JEROME   I said, "Yo, *Kuya,* do you want to go for a ride?" You said no.

JASON   You're not legal!

JEROME   I just wanted to practise for my G2 test.

JASON   Where did you go?

JEROME   Just down the street.

JASON   Liar.

JEROME   I wasn't gone that long.

JASON   You were gone long enough for Ma and Pa to come home from work to an empty driveway. You don't think about anybody but yourself. Where did you go?!

JEROME	Sorry you have to take the bus. It's only a week. You'll live.
JASON	You don't get it.
JEROME	What? What don't I get? You're pissed because you're grounded from the car. You should have just come with me then.
JASON	You think this is just about the car? Tess booked me two gigs for this weekend and now I have to cancel them because of you.
JEROME	Maybe you shouldn't depend on Tess so much.
JASON	Maybe you shouldn't depend on me so much.
JEROME	You're my *kuya*—that's your singular purpose on this earth. And PS, you're not doing a great job at it. I'm still waiting for my birthday present.
JASON	You're so fucken selfish. Europe isn't enough?
JEROME	That's what this is about? You're jealous?
JASON	Get over yourself.
JEROME	How 'bout you let me use your decks for a week and we'll call it even.
JASON	No.
JEROME	Okay, okay, okay. I'll settle for some Tess action.

JASON pushes him.

JASON   Have some respect.

JEROME   Jesus. I'm kidding! I respect you, *Kuya*.

JASON   Yeah? How?

JEROME   Uh . . .

JASON   I wish I wasn't your *kuya*.

JEROME   Done. Whatever you want, Jason. I don't need your *kuya*-ness anyway.

   The bus arrives.

   Uh, *Kuya*, can I borrow a bus ticket?

SCENE 9: BLOG YOU

   The present. JASON'S *room.*

JASON   Two days after the SIU report was released, I created this—

CHORUS   JUSTICE FOR JEROME.

JASON   Because after that first press conference, it just got . . . crazy. Emails, texts, phone calls. Off the chart, you know? After that appearance, everybody was—more than mad. They were outraged. And hungry.

   Just like you. So here is where you meet. Here is where you remember.

JASON's computer screen is projected. He scrolls down the pages and pages of message boards.

CHORUS 2 / 3 I liked him as soon as I heard his Fresh Off The Boat voice—

JEROME reads one in a thick Filipino accent—pronouncing the "f" as a "p."

JEROME My phone number is 555-4455.

CHORUS 2 / 3 I remember his crazy pickup lines—

JEROME *[in a sexy voice]* My phone number is 555-4455.

CHORUS 1 Jer was like my brother. When my parents kicked me out he asked his parents if they could adopt me.

JEROME He can sleep in my bed! I can sleep on the couch.

CHORUS Why you, Jer?
It hurts so much.
I still can't believe it.
I don't want to believe it.

IRENE I love you always and forever. I will always be waiting for the day I will see you again. Love,

[simultaneously] Irene.

JEROME *[simultaneously]* Irene?

Will you go to prom with me?

CHORUS YOUR SON IS SIX FEET UNDER
WITH THREE HOLES IN HIS BACK
AND BOTH OF YOU CRYING IN YOUR BIRD NEST SOUP.
YOUR PUNK KID HAD A KNIFE,
WAS GANGSTER MATERIAL,
THANK GOD HE'S DEAD.
THE POLICE DID THE RIGHT THING,
SHOOT FIRST—ASK LATER.
TAKE CARE
EGG ROLLS

JASON Shit, if you're going to be racist, at least get the race right. I eat *sinigang* not bird's nest. And it's *lumpia* not egg rolls.

JEROME Where are you Nazis? Where are you fags?

JASON You all want to remember. And you all long for the same thing.

CHORUS Tell us the truth.

JASON The truth?

CHORUS Tell us the truth about your brother.

JASON I've told you millions of times—
He played the sax,
Worked at Tim Hortons.
He was a joker,
A pretty good ball player
for 5'4",
An altar boy,
Mom's pride and joy—

CHORUS TELL US THE TRUTH.

JASON   What more do you want?

CHORUS   THE TRUTH.

JASON   Uh . . . I found this assignment Jer wrote for school—

JEROME   I think law enforcement agencies have enough power
         but they need to use it in the proper manner because
         sometimes they tend to pick on people that haven't really
         committed a big crime.

> Transition. PAUL *is hanging out with* JASON *in the
> basement.*

JASON   Paul, check this out.

> JASON *hands* PAUL *the assignment.*

PAUL   Shit. When did he write this?

JASON   Like, two months before the shooting.

PAUL   That's like fucked up, man. Serious.

> JASON *goes to his computer.*

         What are you doing?

JASON   I'm gonna scan it and post it on the site.

PAUL   Why?

JASON   Cuz it's crazy. It's like, foreboding, you know. Like, he knew.
         People are going to go apeshit.

PAUL   Jay, it was just an assignment.

JASON   Yeah. And look, he got an A+ too.

PAUL   So?

JASON   So, it's proof. It's proof he wasn't some delinquent punk-ass
            gangster.

PAUL   Right. Proof.

            So, Jay, are you coming to my bachelor party or what?
            Dean says you haven't replied to his Evite.

JASON   What email did he send it to?

PAUL   You have more than one now?

JASON   Yeah, for the cause, you know. Gives it more credibility
            than a Hotmail address, you know what I mean? Cuz if
            he sent it there, I haven't checked that address in, like,
            forever.

PAUL   Well, it's next Friday. Can you come?

            JASON checks his BlackBerry.

JASON   Aw shit, man. I can't. I'm flying out to Vancouver to make
            a speech to the FilCan Coalition out there.

PAUL   Right. Right.

JASON   You understand, man?

PAUL   Yeah. Sure. It's cool.

JASON   Or at least that's what I think he said.

SCENE 10: THE VIDEO GAME

The present. JASON's *room.*

CHORUS   Tell us the truth!

JASON   Truth? You'll get your truth in four hours. The verdict . . .
            I mean coroner's recommendations . . . at nine a.m.

CHORUS   Tell us the truth!

JASON   He was an altar boy,
            Mom's pride and joy.
            He had dreams of Europe,
            Or the RCMP,
            Or a personality on TV.
            He loved video games—

CHORUS   Truth!

JASON   The day before he was shot, we were just playing video
            games.

            Transition. The past. JASON *and* JEROME *are in the
            basement. They are playing a first-person shooter
            video game.*

JEROME   Eat that, *Kuya!*

JASON   Die. Die. Die!

JEROME   Aw shit, *Kuya*, you didn't have to shoot me point-blank. Where's your heart?

JASON   Don't hate the player.

JEROME   *Kuya*, can I ask you something?

JASON   What?

JEROME   Well, you know, I was thinking about um, options.

JASON   What options?

JEROME   You know, like, post-secondary options.

JASON   Like what, college?

JEROME   No, not really.

JASON   Then what? Spit it out.

JEROME   Do you think Ma and Pa will kill me if I don't go to university?

JASON   Shit, Jer.

JEROME   What?

JASON   What's going on?

JEROME   Nothing. I was thinking maybe university's not for me. Like maybe I need to do something else.

JASON   Like what?

JEROME   I don't know, join the army or the RCMP. I like the RCMP. I like those hats.

JASON   Is this a joke?

JEROME   No.

JASON   You said you were going to university. You told Ma and Pa that it's practically a done deal and that you'll probably even get a scholarship. Did you lie?

JEROME   I didn't lie.

JASON   Your lie is flying you to Europe.

JEROME   What, now you're pissed?

JASON   Jesus, Jer, you're like the last great hope.

JEROME   I want to go. But it's just, well, I'm kinda . . . failing some subjects.

JASON   You just told Ma and Pa that you got an A+ in Media.

JEROME   That's the truth. And I'm killing it in Music. Miss Jack even asked me to help her with the grade nines.

JASON   What's the whole truth, Jer?

JEROME   I'm failing English, Calculus, French, and World Issues.

JASON   World Issues?! Who fails World Issues? Are you retarded?

JEROME	Shut up.
JASON	What's going on, Jer? Is it those friends of yours?
JEROME	Forget it. I shouldn't have said anything.
JASON	Who are those guys anyway? How come I don't see Dean and Vince and Anthony around here anymore?
JEROME	We . . . drifted. Fuck do you care?
JASON	I'm just saying, Jer. I'm hearing things.
JEROME	What?
JASON	That you're hanging out with different people.
JEROME	So? You hardly ever see Paul anymore.
JASON	That's different.
JEROME	Cuz of Tess. Nice, bro. Dump your best friend for some girl.
JASON	Shut up.
JEROME	Don't judge me, *Kuya*.

JEROME's cellphone rings; he answers.

Yo. What up. What? Shit! 'Kay. 'Kay. I'll meet you. I'll be there in thirty minutes.

He hangs up the phone.

I gotta go.

JASON   We're in the middle of the game! You can't leave. That's pussy.

JEROME   Whatever. I gotta go.

Don't tell Ma and Pa about my grades?

JASON   Jer, I'm not going to lie for you.

JEROME   It's not lying. It's buying time.

SCENE II: EVERYBODY LOVES A CHEERLEADER

The past. A rally.

JASON   At first I thought this website would be a place to share memories, feelings, thoughts—you know, commemorate. But this site has become the place for action. The place for momentum. The place for a movement.

CHORUS   SIGN PETITIONS!
CALL YOUR MP!
DEMAND ACTION!

JASON   And every movement needs a leader.

JASON is on a bullhorn at a rally / march.

WHAT DO WE WANT?

CHORUS   TRUTH!

JASON   WHEN DO WE WANT IT?

CHORUS   NOW!

JASON   WHAT DO WE WANT?

CHORUS   JUSTICE!

JASON   WHEN DO WE WANT IT?

CHORUS   NOW!

JASON   WHAT DO WE WANT?

CHORUS   INQUEST!

JASON   WHEN DO WE WANT IT?

CHORUS   NOW!

JASON   My brother was shot in cold blood by a cop one year ago today.

CHORUS   ONE YEAR AND WE STILL FEAR!

JASON   We have been promised an inquest.
When we ask—
When?
They say—
Wait.
And we wait.
And cry ourselves to sleep.
But we don't forget.
And then we ask again—
When?

And they say—
Wait.
And we wait.
And we lose sleep.
But we don't forget.
And then we ask again—
When?
And they say—
Wait.
And I say—
WE ARE WIDE AWAKE!
WE ARE TIRED OF WAITING!

CHORUS   HATE THE WAIT! SET A DATE!

JASON   To the new police chief—
I am calling you out.
Do the right thing.
Restore faith in the system.
Bring trust back between youth and police.

CHORUS   ONE YEAR PAST! INQUEST FAST!

JASON   With each passing day,
The more we wait,
The further we are from the truth.

CHORUS   TELL US THE TRUTH!

          A cellphone rings and rings. TESS *answers it.*

TESS   Jay—

JASON   Not now, Tess—

TESS   / But, Jay.

JASON   I said not now!

TESS   It's the police chief. He wants to meet with you. Tomorrow.

Transition. The POLICE CHIEF'*s office.*

POLICE
CHIEF   On behalf of the Toronto Police Services, I want to offi-
            cially express my condolences to you and your family.

JASON   Uh, thanks. Um, there are some inconsistencies in the
            SIU investigation we'd like to point out to you, sir, and
            we have some specific questions about /

POLICE
CHIEF   I am not able to comment on the specifics. These things
            are best left to the inquest.

JASON   That'll take forever.

POLICE
CHIEF   I empathize with your frustration. I will contact the cor-
            oner's office myself. Immediately. I will urge them to
            expedite the scheduling of the inquest. You have my word.

JASON   How 'bout your apology?

POLICE
CHIEF   I beg your pardon?

JASON   An apology.

POLICE CHIEF	Again, my condolences to you and your family. Thank you for meeting with me.
JASON	Even sympathy is political.

SCENE 12: CELEBRITY

The present. JASON's room. The sounds of email, BlackBerry alerts, phones ringing.

CHORUS 1 This is *The Star.*

CHORUS 2 *The Sun.*

CHORUS 3 *The Globe.*

JASON Being a leader is kind of trippy. I didn't ask for this, but here it is. I've got the papers calling, twenty different social justice groups calling; I'm being asked to speak around the city, across the country, even the mayor's calling. Suddenly, people are listening to me. And because of me, people are taking action.

Both JEROME and JASON are on cellphones.

JEROME Meet behind the ball court at Our Lady of Peace /

JASON Meet in front of City Hall.

JEROME Tell P, Steve, Bryan, Wade, Dean /

JASON   Tell P, Steve, Bryan, Wade, Dean.

JEROME   We'll get back at the Nazis who knocked out Vince's teeth
             and told him to—

CHORUS   Go back where you came from and eat your rice!

JASON   We'll send a message.

JEROME   We'll make them pay.

JASON /
JEROME   We'll make sure nothing like this happens again.

             JASON speaks to the public / press.

JASON   Finally, a year and a half after my brother's death, a date
             has been set for the coroner's inquest.

             CHORUS cheers.

             The last few weeks have been gruelling. We did what we
             had to do. Night and day. Hundreds of phone calls, letters,
             faxes, and emails. It's an encouraging step forward but the
             real battle has only begun.

             CHORUS cheers.

             All we are asking for is the truth to finally come out!

CHORUS   Tell us the truth!
             Tell us the truth!

JASON   Not one eyewitness saw a knife in my brother's hand!

CHORUS   Tell us!

JASON   There was no sign of my brother's fingerprints on the alleged knife!

CHORUS   Tell us!

JASON   So, why did the police need to shoot him three times?

CHORUS   Tell us!

JASON   This inquest will finally reveal the truth behind Jerome's death. I know that my brother is looking down on us from Heaven, smiling. We're making progress, Jer. We'll clear your name yet. We refuse to rest until we achieve justice for Jerome.

            CHORUS cheers.

GIRL   Um, Jason?

JASON   Yeah?

GIRL   Can I get a picture with you?

JASON   Yeah, um, sure.

            He poses with her.

GIRL   I just wanted to tell you that I think you're amazing.

SCENE 13: SPIN

The present. JASON's room.

JASON   Last weekend I went to Paul's wedding. We've been best
         friends since grade five. But his little brother Dean was
         his best man. Dean and Jer were buddies, same age and
         everything. Fuck, if you told me two years ago that Dean
         would be Paul's best man, I'd have called you a dreamer.
         Paul never gave two shits about Dean, could care less if he
         lived or died. Dean was a punk asshole. Maybe he still is.
         I dunno. But to see them there, standing side by side . . .
         I feel robbed.

         *TRANSITION. The past. A concert hall. Loud hip hop
         music plays.*

CHORUS   MAD SKILLZ!

JASON   Two weeks ago—

CHORUS   COME SEE THE T-DOT'S BEST DJS.

JASON   The Filipino associations of three universities organized
         this hip hop DJ fundraising event for the cause.

CHORUS   KILLIN THE DECKS.
         SPINNING FOR JUSTICE.

JASON   I didn't spin.

TESS   Okay, Jay, you're up next right after this set.

JASON   I can't.

TESS   You said you would.

JASON   No. I said I'd speak. I didn't say I'd spin.

TESS   You're billed as Special Guest Appearance. Everyone is expecting you. They're psyched. Are you scared? Is that it?

JASON   I'm not scared.

TESS   Cuz there's nothing to be scared of. You'll be great. You are great. I miss you up there.

JASON   Leave it alone, Tess.

TESS   Jay . . .

JASON   What?

TESS   Jay, I'm trying here.

JASON   Tess, I don't have the time, okay? I could barely fit this. I'll say my speech and then I have to jet. I finally have a meeting with that columnist from *The Star*.

TESS   I can't do this anymore.

JASON   What?

TESS   This.

I need a break.

JASON   What? You're bailing? You're bailing from the cause?

TESS   Look, I know, Jay; I know it's hard. I was there too, remember? I was there at the hospital with you. Jer was like a little brother to me.

JASON   Tess, hell, I don't have time /

TESS   You never have time. No time to spin, no time to see Paul, no time /

JASON   This is my full time job now. Okay? This is bigger than the fucken records. Paul understands. I thought you did too.

TESS   Paul is tired too. We're both tired.

JASON   You're both tired? What, you talk about me?

TESS   Jay, you and I /

JASON   What else are you and Paul doing together?

TESS   What? Are you listening to yourself? Jason, you and I, we don't talk anymore! It's all about Jer.

JASON   That's right, it's all about Jer!

TESS   That's the problem. I'm not bailing on the cause, Jay. I'm bailing on you.

            Shift. JASON's FATHER *enters.*

FATHER   Oh. You're awake.

JASON   Pa? Geez. You scared me.

FATHER   Sorry. Sorry. I couldn't sleep.

JASON   Yeah.

FATHER   Your mom is sleeping. But those pills the doctor gave her to sleep also make her talk in her sleep.

JASON   Right.

FATHER   Your *Tito* Boy called yesterday. He said that he's coming up from Montreal and bringing some friends to support.

JASON   Yeah. I know.

FATHER   Why are you still awake?

JASON   Just updating the website.

FATHER   What are you writing?

JASON   Just. Stuff. Details about the inquest. Inquest stuff.

FATHER   It's good. It's good that you do that.
           I'm glad that you know how to do that . . .

JASON   You should try to get some sleep, Pa. It's a big day tomorrow.

           FATHER moves to leave.

FATHER   Jason?

JASON   Yeah?

FATHER   Your brother. He was a good boy, wasn't he?

JASON   Yeah, Pa. The best.

SCENE 14: FRONT PAGE

The past. A newsroom.

CHORUS   EXCLUSIVE!

JASON   Two years after the altercation—

ANCHOR   The coroner's inquest into the tragic death of seventeen-year-old Jerome De Jesus starts today.

JASON   —my brother makes the front page. And so do I.

ANCHOR   In this exclusive interview, we asked his older brother, Jason De Jesus, what this means to him and his family.

JASON   We have been waiting a very long time for this. Our hope—myself, my family, and all our supporters—is to prevent other children, other young women and men, from dying the same way that my brother died. This should not have happened to my brother and it should not happen to anyone else ever again. Justice for Jerome equals justice for all.

ANCHOR   What do you expect will happen at the inquest?

JASON   For obvious reasons, we don't completely trust the evidence put forth by the police. We conducted our own private investigation. The indisputable, consistent facts are—

CHORUS   ONE

JASON   The officers were in plain clothes and not in uniform.

CHORUS   TWO

JASON   Eyewitnesses said that no knife was ever seen in Jerome's hands.

CHORUS   THREE

JASON   The SIU did not arrive at the scene until two hours after the fact.

CHORUS   FOUR

JASON   A knife was found at the scene but had no fingerprints or blood on it whatsoever.

CHORUS   FIVE

JASON   Reports say that Officer X has a history of excessive and violent force on young people.

CHORUS   SIX

JASON   Officer X has been cleared of any wrongdoing and is armed and back to work in Toronto.

ANCHOR   Are you implying that the police planted the knife?

JASON   Let me just say that we've been waiting two years for this inquest, and I am confident that the truth, the whole ugly truth, will be revealed.

SCENE 15: REPLAY

Twenty-seven seconds are projected counting down.
It counts down slowly, not in real time.

CHORUS   VERSION TWO.
I'm being chased!
TEN
TWELVE
FOURTEEN
SIXTEEN
EIGHTEEN
TWENTY
FIFTY
Brown boys
Carrying bats
Crutches
Batons
Guns
Knives—
I'm outnumbered.

The sound of throwing up.

All units,
All units,
Reports of gang activity.

JEROME   Where are you fags?! Where are you Nazis?!

OFFICER X   Police. Drop the rock.

JEROME   Who the fuck are you?

> *JEROME turns around and begins to walk away, still holding the rock.*

OFFICER X   You are under arrest for possession of a dangerous weapon.

JEROME   Get off of me, you fat pig!

> *OFFICER X pins JEROME to the ground, one knee behind his back, the other on his shoulder, and attempts to cuff his wrists.*

Aughh!

> *JEROME screams / struggles / strikes out.*

OFFICER X   HE'S GOT A KNIFE!

> *Pop. Pop. Pop.*

SCENE 16: HE SPEAKS

The past. At the inquest.

REPORTER   Emotions ran high today—

JASON   Two days ago—

REPORTER   —as the officer who shot Jerome De Jesus took the stand.

JASON   —for the first time ever—

OFFICER X   My name is Constable Donald Grainger.

JASON   —I heard his voice.

OFFICER X   I can't sleep.
I haven't.
I don't know how long it's been.

The last thing that I wanted to do was use my weapon
that day.
I am haunted every single day, every single night.
There was no other alternative.

MOTHER   Killer cop!

OFFICER X   There was no other way.
He had a knife.
I had to stop him.
There was no other way.

REPORTER   There is nothing that the officer can say that will appease
this family. Nothing short of Constable Grainger behind
bars can calm their rage. This inquest has been mostly
about the cops and what happened in the span of twenty-
seven seconds. But De Jesus is dead and overwhelming
testimony has shown that he was no innocent bystander.
And that's the ugly truth that no family wants to face.

JASON   Fuck you.

SCENE 17: KIDS

Present. JASON's *room.*

CHORUS   TELL US THE TRUTH!

JASON   Fuck that reporter and her easy words.

CHORUS   TELL US!

JASON   What more do you want?

CHORUS   THE TRUTH!

JASON   Let me think—

CHORUS   TELL US!

JASON   Okay, like, say Jer really did have a rock. Say he really
             did have a knife, even. Say he struggled to get on his feet.
             Maybe he even took a swipe.

CHORUS   TELL US THE TRUTH!
             Tell us the truth!

JASON   Say all that shit really happened. Imagine it.
             Got it? Got it in your head?
             Can you picture it?
             Now picture this.
             Kids.
             Just kids.
             Don't think a bunch of thugs,
             Don't think gangs,

Think—
Kids.
Try hard. Just because they're fifteen, sixteen, seventeen
years old, they're still kids.
You were one. I was one.
Think about every time you and a bunch of guys got into
a brawl at school.

Over some girl.
Over some shit piece of gossip.
Over a fucken basketball.
Over anything.

CHORUS   TRUTH!
            TRUTH!
            TELL US THE TRUTH!

JASON   Hold on, fuck, I'm getting to it.
            Look, I'm trying to say—
            Fights happen.
            Fights between kids happen all the time.
            And happen everywhere.
            Not just in Scarborough. Don't tell me there's never been
            a fight at Rosedale Heights or Cardinal Carter or fucken
            Upper Canada College or whatever.

CHORUS   TRUTH!

JASON   Fuck. Hold up! Even though the newspapers may make
            you believe that every fight ends up with a shooting or a
            death, it's not the whole truth. Because it doesn't always
            end up that way. Hell, you're still alive. I'm still alive. Some
            kid may get a bloody lip, a broken arm, okay, maybe even
            end up in the hospital.

CHORUS   TELL US THE TRUTH!

JASON   But it's just between kids and kids.
And then—
The cops show up.
They don't see just kids.
They see—
Jane and Finch Kids.
Clarkson Kids.
Tuxedo Court Kids.
Bendale Kids.
Crescent Town Kids.
Galloway Kids.

Not—
Kids who have parents,
Who have futures,
Who have families who love them.
They show up to stop a fight,
They don't know if it's
Over some girl
Or some shit piece of gossip
Or a fucken basketball.
Because they don't ask—

JEROME enters.

Why did you go?
Why did you go with them?
Why couldn't you just leave it alone?

OFFICER X enters.

To them it's a situation.
To them it's an incident.

To them it's an altercation.
They show up—
Not with pepper spray
Or batons
Or tasers, even.
But with guns.

And suddenly it changes.
Suddenly it's some kind of social problem.
Suddenly it's an issue.
Suddenly it's political.
Suddenly it's a headline.
Suddenly it's a bill that needs to get passed.
Suddenly it's a law that needs to get changed.
Suddenly it's a cause.
Suddenly it's an inquest.
Suddenly—

Twenty-seven seconds are projected counting down.
This time it is actually twenty-seven seconds. We sit
in real time for every second.

OFFICER X   Pop! Pop! Pop!

JASON   And suddenly here I am being a spokesperson instead of
a brother.

I'm just saying.

SCENE 18: FIGHT THE POWER

The present. JASON's *room.*

CHORUS   TELL US!
       TELL US!

JASON   I did. I just did.

CHORUS   TELL US /

JASON   He loved video games.
       He loved music and records,
       And his family.
       He was my /

CHORUS   THE TRUTH!

JASON   Truth? I'll tell you the truth.
       The truth is Officer . . . Grainger . . . shot my brother.
       And my brother is dead.
       And I'm angry and I'm tired and I'm spinning out of control instead of on my decks.
       I drove away my girl and I shut out my best friend /

CHORUS   THE TRUTH!

JASON   But the whole truth?
       The whole damn truth is
       The day my brother was shot
       I found it. I found the record.

Transition. The past. JASON's *room.* JEROME *is playing
a video game on the couch.* JASON *enters.*

JEROME Yo, wanna play?

JASON No. I'm spinning downtown tonight. I'm late. I still have
to pick up Tess.

JEROME Cool. Where?

JASON At her house, stupid.

JEROME Where are you spinning?

JASON Fluid.

JEROME Can I come?

JASON It's not all-ages.

JEROME I have ID.

JASON I'm not aiding and abetting you tonight.

JEROME Jeez, *Kuya*, *Tito* Boy used to take you before you were
legal.

JASON Then ask *Tito* Boy.

JEROME *Kuya* . . .

JASON I don't have time to fight with you tonight, Jer.

JEROME's phone rings.

JEROME	Yo. Now? Where did you see them? Okay. I'm on my way. I'll meet you at the ball court.

JEROME moves to leave. JASON goes to retrieve his gear and discovers that his favourite record is spinning on the turntable.

JASON	What the hell? Jer!
JEROME	What?
JASON	WHAT THE FUCK IS THIS?
JEROME	Uh, your deck?
JASON	The record. Were you messing with my gear?
JEROME	No.

JASON removes the record from the turntable.

JASON	Jesus Christ, it's scratched!
JEROME	*[under breath]* Shit.
JASON	YOU FUCKEN ASSHOLE! DO YOU KNOW HOW MUCH THIS IS WORTH?!
JEROME	I didn't touch it.
JASON	I'm tired of your lies.
JEROME	Who's lying? I don't know what you're talking about.
JASON	QUIT LYING!

JEROME   Maybe you left it there last night—

JASON   For real?

JEROME   Okay, it was me. I was just messing. Sorry. I gotta go.

           JEROME leaves.

CHORUS   TELL US THE TRUTH!

           Rewind.

JASON   For real?

JEROME   Okay, it was me. I was just messing. Sorry. I gotta go.

JASON   Fuck you and your easy words, Jer. Not this time.

JEROME   *Kuya*, it was an accident. I have to go.

           Shift.

JASON   Stay.

JEROME   What? Get out of the way, *Kuya*.

JASON   Stay.

JEROME   I gotta go!

JASON   Where? Where are you going?

JEROME   Those fucken white guys at the ball court knocked Vince's teeth out yesterday. We're going to take care of them.

JASON   Don't go.

JEROME   I gotta go.

JEROME leaves.

CHORUS   THE TRUTH!

Rewind.

JASON   For real?

JEROME   Okay, it was me. I was just messing. Sorry.

JASON shuts down, goes about his business, packing his gear.

Kuya, it was an accident. Sorry.

JEROME blocks JASON from leaving.

I said sorry, *Kuya*. Geez.

JASON   Get out of my way before I fucken kill you.

JEROME   Whatever.

JASON, provoked, drops his gear and charges JEROME. JEROME throws a punch. They fight. JEROME pins JASON. JASON struggles and gets up.

JASON   Fuck you.

CHORUS   THE TRUTH!

Rewind.

JASON   I hate you.

CHORUS   THE TRUTH!

Rewind.

JASON   I wish you were never born.

SCENE 19: CHANGE THE ENDING

The present. JASON's *room.*

CHORUS   Truth.

JASON   I can't sleep.
I haven't.
I don't know how long it's been.
I don't deserve it.

In a few hours the coroner's inquest will reconvene, and
a panel of strangers will make a recommendation.

In few hours, you'll get some sound bites.
You can log off. You can walk away.
You can go to sleep thinking—
Tsk tsk, what a shame.

No matter what the outcome—
You get a hero.

You're welcome.

CHORUS   Truth.

JASON   Truth?
I don't fucken care.
Nothing's gonna bring back my brother.
Nothing's gonna take back the last thing I ever said to him.
He's dead.

JEROME appears. JASON sees him.

In all the times people asked me about Jer, they never asked about me and Jer. Like they wanted to know what kind of son he was and uncle he was and friend he was. But nobody asked what kind of brother he was. Nobody asked what kind of brother I was. If you asked me I'd say I was shit, man. I was shit.

Do me a favour, don't ask.
Nobody needs to know. All you need to know is—

CHORUS   He played the sax,
Worked at Tim Hortons.
He was a joker,
A pretty good ball player
for 5'4",
An altar boy,
Mom's pride and joy.
He had dreams of Europe,
Or the RCMP,
Or a personality on TV.
He loved video games.
He loved music and records,
And his family—

JASON What does it really matter? How's it gonna make you sleep better to know where he worked or what he wanted to be when he grew up?

JASON [*simultaneously*] Truth?

JEROME [*simultaneously*] Truth.

JASON He was a kid. Just a kid.
You can make a martyr of him if you want.
Hell, I'll help you. But, fuck. The plain and simple truth is he was just a kid.

And he should be alive.

Shift. A Christmas that should have been.

JEROME Hey, *Kuya*!

JASON Jer?

JEROME Merry Christmas.

JEROME hands JASON the wrapped record.

JASON [*without opening it*] Thanks, dick.

THE END

ACKNOWLEDGEMENTS

The development of this play was made possible by the generous support of the Toronto Arts Council [TAC] and the Ontario Arts Council [OAC].

The play received formative development during a playwright residency with fu-GEN Asian Canadian Theatre Company, made possible through the Ontario Arts Council.

Additional support from the OAC was made possible by Roseneath Theatre, Cahoots Theatre Company, Young People's Theatre, Carousel Players, and Buddies in Bad Times Theatre through the Theatre Creators' Reserve Program.

The development of this play would not have been possible without the workshop support of David S. Craig, Dave Carley, Nina Lee Aquino, Roseneath Theatre, fu-GEN Asian Canadian Theatre Company, and Canadian Stage.

The playwright is grateful for the wonderful actors who have participated in the development of the play: Sean Baek, Michaela Washburn, Sarah Henriques, Christian Feliciano, Kimwun Perehinec, Sharmila Dey, Grant Tilly, Richard Lee, Aura Carcueva, Madeleine Donohue, Keith Barker, Sharon Marquez, Byron Abalos, Mike Realba, Darrel Gamotin, Christine Mangosing, Paul Sun-Hyung Lee, Tara Beagan, Rose Cortez, Reese Baguio, Vince Galvez, Colin Doyle, Leah-Simone

Bowen, Andre Wilson, Jackie Caballero, Andrew Pimento, Roberto Martinez, and Tashauna Clarke.

Thank you Annie Gibson, Blake Sproule, Christine Mangosing, and the Playwrights Canada Press team for your editorial insights, support, creativity, and patience in the publication of this play.

Heart-filled love and gratitude to Paul Parker—who saved me from writer's block by reminding me that Jeffrey was just a kid.

And lastly, thank you to the Reodica family, especially Joel Reodica. You are heroes.

Marie Beath Badian is a Toronto-based playwright, performer, director, and arts educator. Her other plays include *Prairie Nurse*, *Mind Over Matter*, and *Novena*. Her radio work includes *Yellow Rubber Boots* (CBC *Outfront*) and an adaption of *Novena* (CBC Radio—*The Drama of Immigration*). Marie Beath has been playwright-in-residence at fu-GEN Asian Canadian Theatre Company and Project: Humanity. She was a member of the 2010 Hot House Creators Unit at Cahoots Theatre Company, the 2013–14 Playwrights Unit at Tarragon Theatre, the 2015 Soulpepper Playwrights Circle, and the 2015–16 Natural Resources creation group at Factory Theatre.

First edition: February 2017
Printed and bound in Canada by Imprimerie Gauvin, Gatineau

Cover design by Christine Mangosing // CMANGO Design
Author photo © Christian Lloyd // Getting Captured

**PLAYWRIGHTS
CANADA PRESS**

202-269 Richmond St. W.
Toronto, ON
M5V 1X1

416.703.0013
info@playwrightscanada.com
www.playwrightscanada.com
@playcanpress

A **bundled** eBook edition is available
with the purchase of this print book.

CLEARLY PRINT YOUR NAME ABOVE IN UPPER CASE

Instructions to claim your eBook edition:
1. Download the BitLit app for Android or iOS
2. Write your name in **UPPER CASE** above
3. Use the BitLit app to submit a photo
4. Download your eBook to any device

MIX
Paper
FSC FSC® C100212